YOUTH

JUL 0 4 2001

Milford Sound On
South Island

FACES
AND
PLACES

NEW ZEALAND

BY PATRICK RYAN

THE CHILD'S WORLD®, INC.

Area: Two islands that total 104,000 square miles—about as big as Colorado.

Population: About 4 million people.

Capital City: Wellington.

Other Important Cities: Auckland, Christchurch, Dunedin.

Money: The New Zealand dollar.

National Languages: English and Maori.

National Sport: Rugby.

National Holiday: Waitangi Day on February 6.

Important Holiday: The Queen of England's Birthday (the first Monday in June).

National Flag: Blue with the flag of Great Britain in the upper left corner. There are also stars on the flag. The stars represent a group of real stars in the night sky called the *Southern Cross.*

Library of Congress Cataloging-in-Publication Data
Ryan, Pat (Patrick M.)
New Zealand / by Patrick Ryan.
Series: "Faces and Places".
p. cm.
Includes index.
Summary: Describes the geography, history, people, and culture of the mountainous island country of New Zealand.
ISBN 1-56766-577-2 (library : reinforced : alk. paper)

1. New Zealand — Juvenile literature.
[1. New Zealand] I. Title.

DU408.R93 1999
993 — dc21

98-11692
CIP
AC

GRAPHIC DESIGN
Robert A. Honey, Seattle

PHOTO RESEARCH
James R. Rothaus / James R. Rothaus & Associates

ELECTRONIC PRE–PRESS PRODUCTION
Robert E. Bonaker / Graphic Design & Consulting Co.

PHOTOGRAPHY
Cover photo: Young Rugby Players
by Kevin Fleming/Corbis

Table
of
Contents

If you were on the Space Shuttle looking down on Earth, you would see large pieces of land called **continents**. Continents can be found all over the planet. As you look at Earth, imagine that you could cut it in half. The halves are called **hemispheres**.

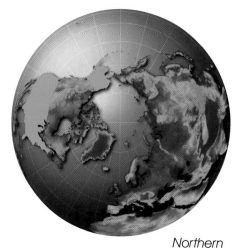

Northern Hemisphere

Southern Hemisphere

New Zealand (white) is in the south and U.S.A. (green) is in the north.

The top half of the world is called the northern hemisphere. The bottom half is called the southern

hemisphere. Australia is one of the continents that can be found in the southern hemisphere. Just east of Australia, there are two large islands. This is the country of New Zealand.

The World Shown Flat

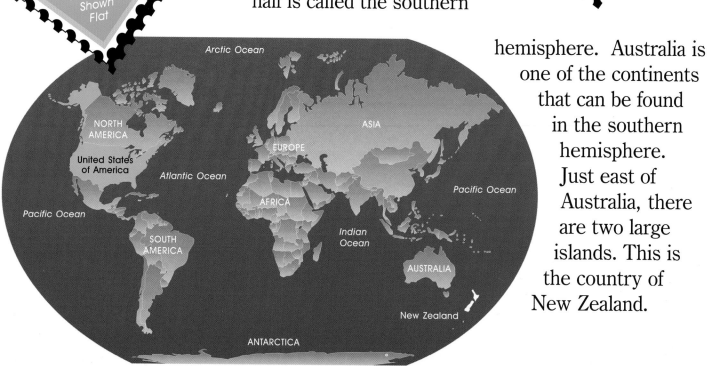

Arctic Ocean

NORTH AMERICA

United States of America

Atlantic Ocean

Pacific Ocean

SOUTH AMERICA

ASIA

EUROPE

AFRICA

Indian Ocean

Pacific Ocean

AUSTRALIA

New Zealand

ANTARCTICA

Close-Up of New Zealand

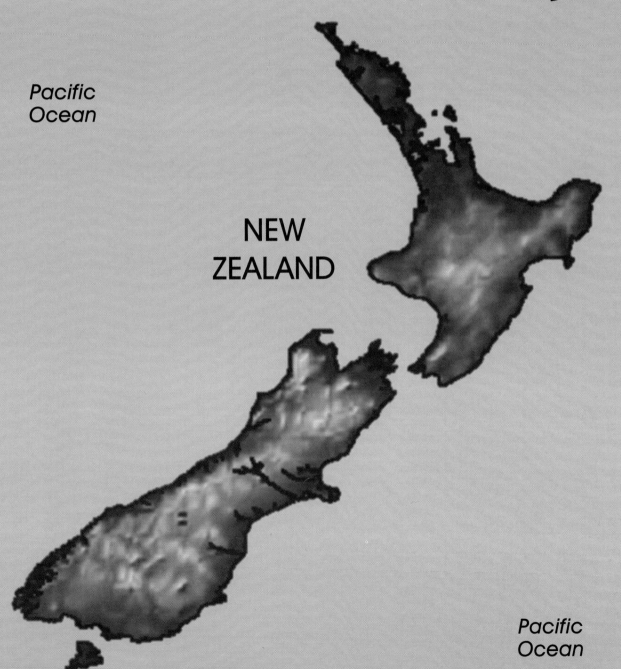

Pacific
Ocean

NEW
ZEALAND

Pacific
Ocean

Mount Cook
And The
Southern
Alps

Cathedral Cove Beach

NORTH ISLAND

Mount Cook
Southern Alps
Doubtful Sound
SOUTH ISLAND

Robert Dowling/Corbis

The Land

New Zealand is made up of two main parts—the North Island and the South Island. There are also many smaller islands, but not many people live there. One thing that you are sure to find in New Zealand is mountains— they can be found almost everywhere!

Jack Fields/Corbis

Waterfall Above Doubtful Sound, South Island

On the North Island, there is a lot of rich farmland and green forests. There are also volcanoes. The South Island is larger than the North Island. It also has thick forests and tall mountains. In fact, 17 of the mountains on New Zealand's South Island are over 10,000 feet tall! They are called the *Southern Alps*.

Farmland And Hills On The North Island

Corel Galleria™

Greg Probst/Corbis

Cathedral Cove Beach, North Island

Plants & Animals

ADMIT ONE ADMIT ONE

Herd Of Deer On South Island

Craig Lovell/Corbis

New Zealand could be called the land of mysterious plants. That's because there are more than 2,000 kinds, or **species**, that live there. New Zealand's plants are very special. In fact, about 1,500 of the plants that grow there cannot be found anywhere else in the world. Mamku and whekiponga plants grow in many places. Trees such as the kauri rimu and the totara live there, too.

Most of the animals of New Zealand started out as visitors. They were brought to the islands many years ago by settlers from other continents. Deer, weasels, opossums and rabbits all came to New Zealand with new settlers and their boats.

The most famous bird in New Zealand is called a *kiwi*. It makes its home in the green forests of the islands. Kiwi birds have long beaks and a good sense of smell. They are different from many other birds because they cannot fly.

Waipoua Kauri Forest Reserve, New Zealand

Pukeko Wades In Shallow Water

Paul A. Souders/©Corbis

Geoff Moon; Frank Lane Picture Agency/Corbis

10

SOUTH ISLAND

Riponui Reserve Waipoua Kauri Forest Reserve

Brown Kiwi
In Riponui
Reserve

Bay of Islands

Auckland

Maori War Dancers

Bay Of Island's 1840 Waitangi Treaty House

Long Ago

According to legend, New Zealand was first discovered by an explorer named Kupe. Kupe's canoe arrived in New Zealand sometime around the year 900. He was a member of a group of people called the *Maori* (m–OW–ree). The early Maori people were fierce warriors. They were highly organized and skilled in many crafts. The Maori liked the islands and settled there.

1770 Engraving Of James Cook

Library of Congress/Corbis

In 1642, a Dutch explorer named Abel Tasman saw New Zealand's islands from his ship. Even though he thought the lands were beautiful, he did not go ashore—he was afraid of the Maori! Finally, in 1769, a British explorer named Captain Cook arrived in New Zealand and opened the islands to be settled by other countries. By 1840, the country of England ruled New Zealand.

Maori War Dancers Make Faces At Enemies

1853 View Of Auckland

Dave G. Houser/Corbis

Illustrated London News/Corbis

Today, New Zealand has its own government. They have their own laws and rules. They even have their own flag. Even so, New Zealand still has close ties with the country of England. In fact, New Zealand recognizes the Queen of England as one of their official leaders.

Neil Rabinowitz/Corbis

The Maori people have not been forgotten, either. Many Maori help make laws and rules that protect their native peoples and lands. They also work hard to protect New Zealand and the many plants and animals that live there.

1990 Visit Of Queen Elizabeth II

Painted Maori Making Demands At Waitangi

Christchurch Town Hall

Neil Rabinowitz/Corbis

Dsve G. Houser/Corbis

Waitangi

★ Wellington

Christchurch

Paul A. Souders/© Corbis

The Beehive,
Seat Of
Parliament,
Wellington

Period
Costumes
At Cricket
Match
In Waitangi

•Waitangi

NORTH ISLAND

•Rotorua

•Levin

STEWART ISLAND

The People

About 4 million people live in New Zealand. Most of them live on the North Island. Many New Zealanders are relatives of the early settlers and explorers from other countries. Others belong to the Maori people.

Many **immigrants** also live in New Zealand. They are people who moved from other countries to live in New Zealand. Many immigrants come to New Zealand from countries such as India and China.

Grandson Of One Of The First Whalers, Lives On Stewart Island

James L. Amos/Corbis

Immigrant Chinese Farmers Near Levin

Paul A. Souders/©Corbis

Maori Woodcarver From Rotorua

Dave G. Houser/Corbis

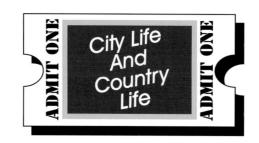

ADMIT ONE

City Life
And
Country
Life

ADMIT ONE

Most of New Zealand's people live in cities. Auckland and Wellington are the two big cities on the North Island. Christchurch and Dunedin are the big cities on the South Island. Wellington is the **capital city** of the whole country. It is located on the coast between the two islands.

Queen Street In Auckland

Michael S. Yamashita/Corbis

New Zealand's cities are much like those in the United States. There are buildings, shops, and busy streets. There are restaurants and hotels, too. City people live in houses or apartments called *flats*. Many drive cars or ride buses to go places.

The countryside of New Zealand is much calmer. The people there live on small farms or in little towns. Many are farmers that raise sheep in large fields.

Wellington Harbor

Paul A. Souders/© Corbis

Cottage Near Nelson Lakes National Park

Adam Woolfitt/Corbis

18

Auckland

NORTH ISLAND

Nelson Lakes
National Park ☆ Wellington

Christchurch

SOUTH ISLAND

Dunedin

Wolfgang Kaehler/Corbis

Cathedral
Square
In
Christchurch

Christ's
College Boys
Wear
Traditional
Uniforms

Auckland
Napier
Christchurch

James L. Amos/Corbis

Schools And Language

Children in New Zealand start school when they are about five or six years old. They learn math, reading, and writing, just as you do. At some New Zealand schools, students must wear uniforms. At other schools, children can wear regular clothes.

Howard Davies/Corbis

Iraqi Immigrants Studying In Auckland

New Zealand has two official languages, English and Maori. The Maori language is used in ceremonies and special occasions. Some Maori words can even be found in English. *Kiwi* is one Maori word that many people use every day.

School Uniforms Known As "Zebra Suits"

Kevin Fleming/Corbis

Kevin Fleming/Corbis

Private School Only For Maoris In Napier

New Zealanders work at many different jobs. Some people work in the cities at big companies. Others work in restaurants or small shops. Farming and raising animals in New Zealand are very important jobs, too. The mild weather is perfect for growing crops or raising huge herds of sheep and cows.

Paul A. Souders/© Corbis

Lettuce Harvest Near Levin

Another important job in New Zealand is **tourism**. In this job, New Zealanders show visitors from other places about their country. They show people their beautiful forests and wild animals. They also show them the busy cities. Each year, more and more travelers come to New Zealand to enjoy its natural beauty and clean environment.

Woman Working In Dunedin Wool Factory

James L. Amos/Corbis

Patrick Ward/Corbis

Tourists On Southern Alps

James L. Amos/Corbis

Levin

SOUTH ISLAND

Southern Alps

Dunedin

Shearing
Sheep On
South
Island

Dining Out
On South
Island

Auckland   Devonport

SOUTH ISLAND

Food

New Zealanders enjoy many of the same foods that we do. They also have many neat dishes of their own. Many New Zealanders like to eat tea and *biscuits* in the middle of the afternoon. Biscuits are another name for cookies—and some of them are covered in milk chocolate!

Many people in New Zealand like to eat **mutton**, or roasted lamb. It is used in lots of dishes, from soup to sandwiches. Another favorite dish is the meat pie. It has a flaky crust and is filled with things such as meat or vegetables.

Fish And Chips In Auckland

Robert Holmes/Corbis

Sheepshearers Lunch Break

James L. Amos/Corbis

Picnic On A Park Bench In Devonport

Paul A. Souders/©Corbis

There is one word for sports in New Zealand—rugby. New Zealanders love to play it and watch it, too. The national New Zealand rugby team is called the All Blacks. They get their name from the fact that they wear all-black uniforms. They are considered to be one of the strongest rugby teams in the world.

When they are not playing rugby, many people spend time doing other things outdoors. In the mountains, people often go hiking, camping, skiing, and snowboarding. At the sea, people go fishing, swimming, and sailing.

Kevin Fleming/Corbis

Rugby Players Start Young In Christchurch

Ironman Surfing Finals At Mount Maunganui

Patrick Ward/Corbis

Horse Racing At Gore

Paul A. Souders/©Corbis

Mount Maunganui •

• Christchurch

■ Marion Lake

• Gore

Galen Rowell/Corbis

Hiking
Above
Marion
Lake

Maori Culture
Group At
Waitangi Day
Celebration

Waitangi

Milford Sound

Paul A. Souders/©Corbis

Beautiful Milford Sound

Vic Sievey; Eye Ubiquitous/Corbis

New Zealanders have many holidays, such as Christmas and New Year's. They also celebrate holidays that can only be found in New Zealand. At the beginning of June, New Zealanders celebrate the birthday of the Queen of England. On April 25, New Zealanders honor the people who fought during the two World Wars.

Queen Elizabeth II's Birthday Is Celebrated Each Year

UPI/Corbis-Bettman

New Zealand is a wonderful country full of strange plants and towering mountains. Its beautiful countryside and mild weather make it a perfect vacation spot. The people of New Zealand are happy and kind—and they are ready for you to come and visit one day!

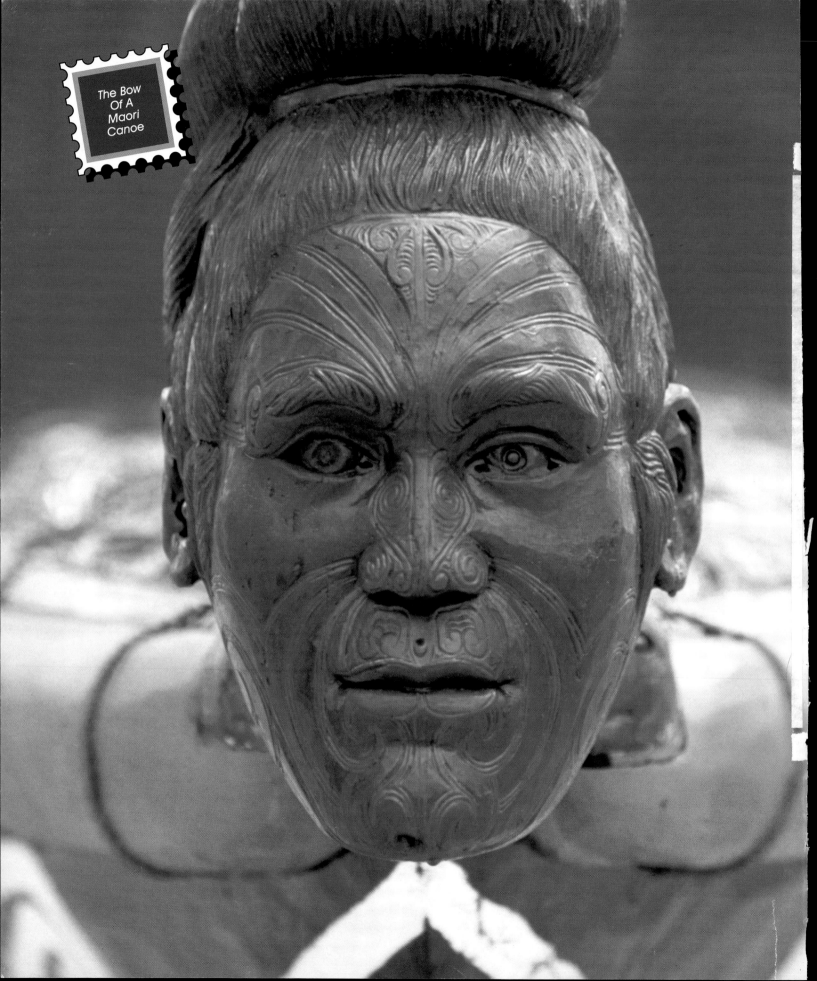

The seasons of the year happen at opposite times in Earth's hemispheres. When the countries in the northern hemisphere are having springtime, those in the southern hemisphere are getting ready for winter. Since New Zealand is in the southern hemisphere, Christmas happens in the middle of summer!

When water flows down a drain in New Zealand, it swirls to the left. In the United States, it swirls to the right.

New Zealand is one of the closest countries to Antarctica. Many polar travelers stop off at New Zealand's Stewart Island before heading for the South Pole.

Long ago, the largest birds on Earth lived in New Zealand. These birds, called moas, often grew to be 12 feet tall.

How Do You Say?

	MAORI	HOW TO SAY IT
Hello	kia ora	(key–or–ra)
Goodbye	haere ra	(high–re–rah)
Please	whakawaireka	(far–car–why–rek–ka)
Thank You	kia ora	(key–or–ra)
One	taha	(tah–HAH)
Two	rua	(roo–AH)
Three	toru	(toh–roo)
New Zealand	Aotearoa	(ah–OH–te–ah–row–ah)

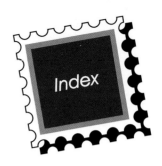

capital city (KAP–ih–tull SIH–tee)
A capital city is where all of the government offices for a country can be found. New Zealand's capital city is Wellington.

continent (KON–tuh–nent)
All the land areas on Earth are divided up into huge sections called continents. Most of the continents are separated by oceans.

hemisphere (HEM–is–sfeer)
Earth is divided into two halves called hemispheres. New Zealand is in the southern hemisphere.

immigrants (IM–ih–grant)
An immigrant is a newcomer from another country. Some New Zealanders are immigrants.

mutton (MUH–tun)
Mutton is meat from sheep. Many New Zealand dishes are made with mutton.

species (SPEE–sheez)
A species is a different kind of a plant or animal. There are more than 2,000 species of plants in New Zealand.

tourism (TOOR–ih–zem)
The business of showing travelers around a country is called tourism. Tourism is a very important business in New Zealand.